I'm going to eat this ANT

For Rafaël, Lucille and Marylène, with lots of love

Bloomsbury Publishing, London, Oxford, New York, New Delhi and Sydney

First published in Great Britain in 2017 by Bloomsbury Publishing Plc
50 Bedford Square, London, WC1B 3DP

www.bloomsbury.com

BLOOMSBURY is a registered trademark of Bloomsbury Publishing Plc

Text and illustrations © Chris Naylor-Ballesteros 2017
The moral rights of the author/illustrator have been asserted

A CIP catalogue record of this book is available from the British Library

ISBN 978 1 4088 6989 5 (HB)   ISBN 978 1 4088 6990 1 (PB)   ISBN 978 1 4088 7387 8 (eBook)

All papers used by Bloomsbury Publishing are natural, recyclable products made from wood grown in well managed forests.
The manufacturing processes conform to the environmental regulations of the country of origin

Printed in China by C & C Offset Printing Co Ltd, Shenzhen, Guangdong

1 3 5 7 9 10 8 6 4 2

I'm going to eat this ANT

CHRIS NAYLOR-BALLESTEROS

BLOOMSBURY
LONDON OXFORD NEW YORK NEW DELHI SYDNEY

Ants, ants, ants . . . and *more* ants!

I've just about had enough of licking up

wriggling, tickling, stinging,

fighting, BITING ants

with my twisting twirling tongue.

The problem is this . . .

I'm hungry.

What's an anteater to do?

I know! For a change, I think

I'm going to eat . . .

THIS
ant . . .

. . . served in a sandwich

or sucked up a straw.

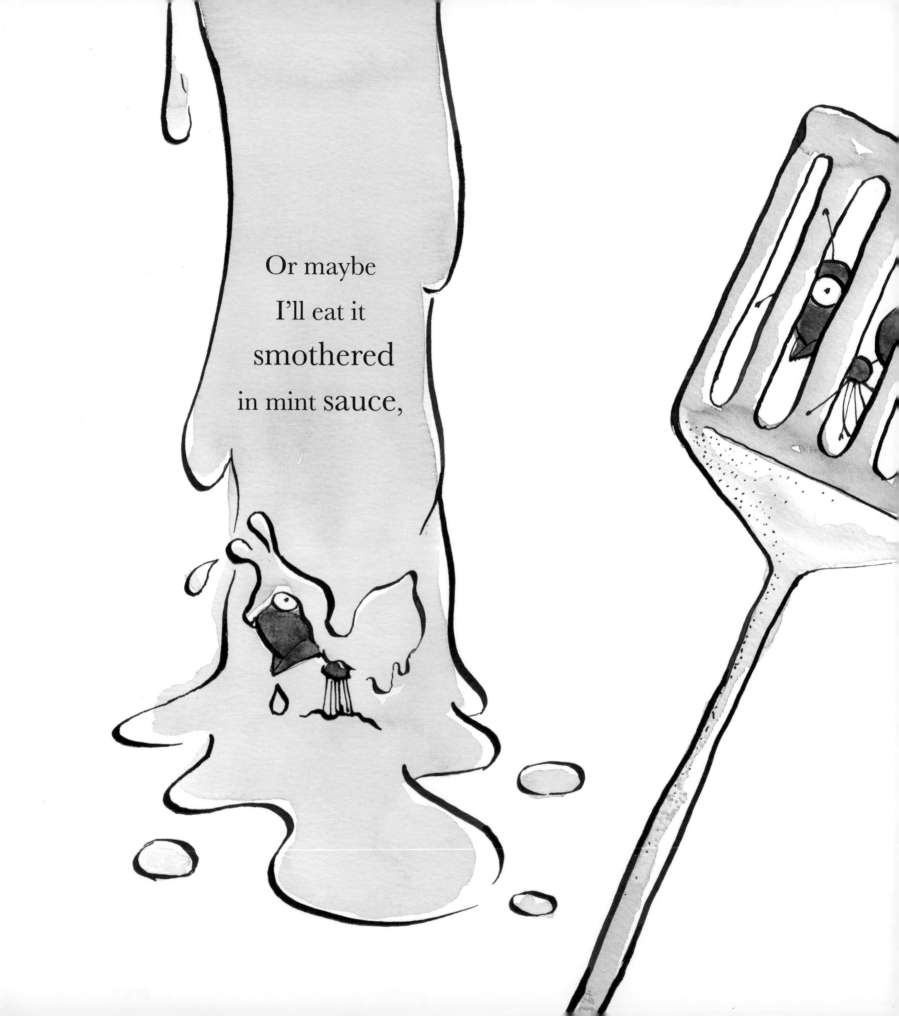

Or maybe
I'll eat it
smothered
in mint sauce,

or splattered
with a
spatula

or simmering in soup
and scooped in a spoon.

Perhaps sundried
or salted,

or sliced like salami
(any of these would be nice).

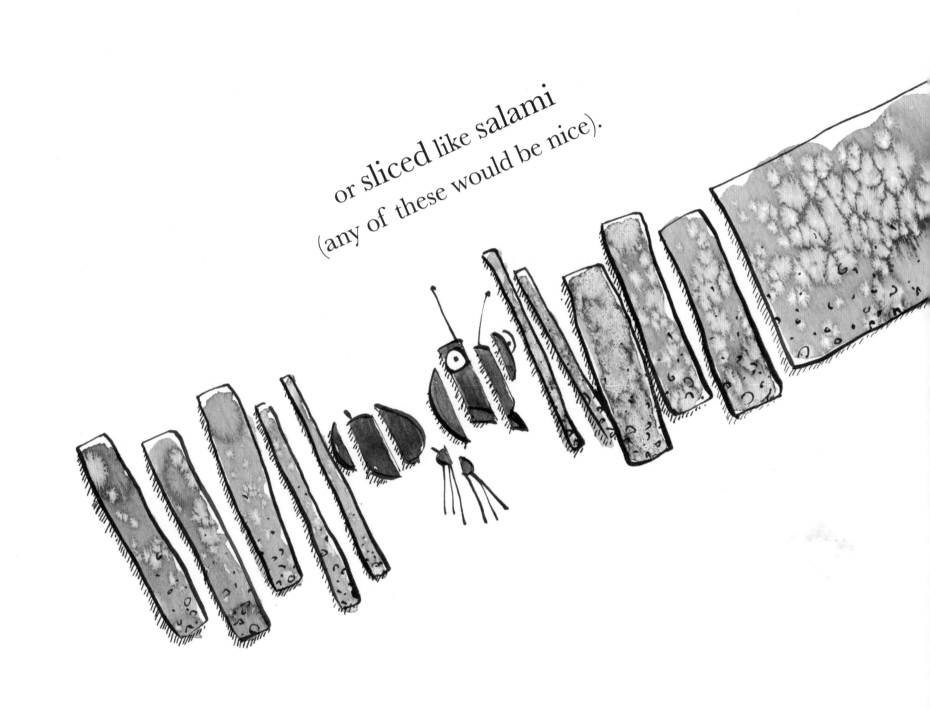

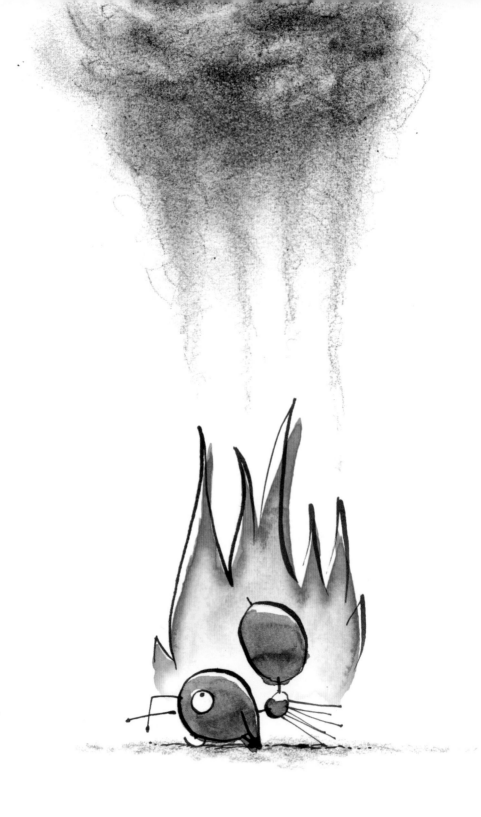

How about seared like steak?

Speared
on a
stick?

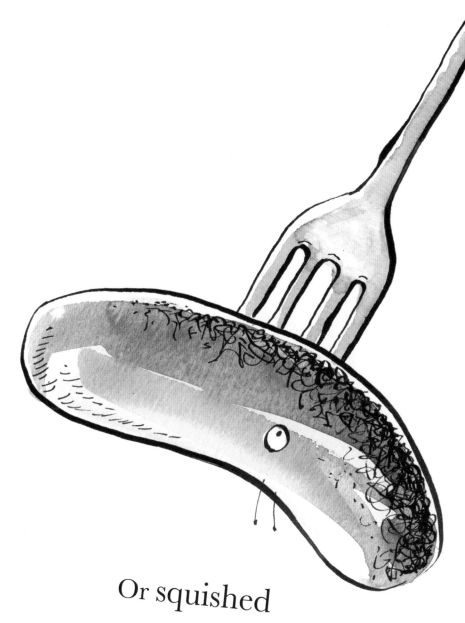

Or squished
in a sausage?

Or maybe smoked with sardines,

stir fried

and sautéed?

And for dessert, I could have it

set in a sorbet . . .

Or stuck on a sweet.

Mmmmmmmmmmmmmm!

So many savoury,
spicy, sugary
snacks . . .

Which scrumptious serving should I scoff?

Let's see . . .

Hang on . . .

Where *is* THAT ant?

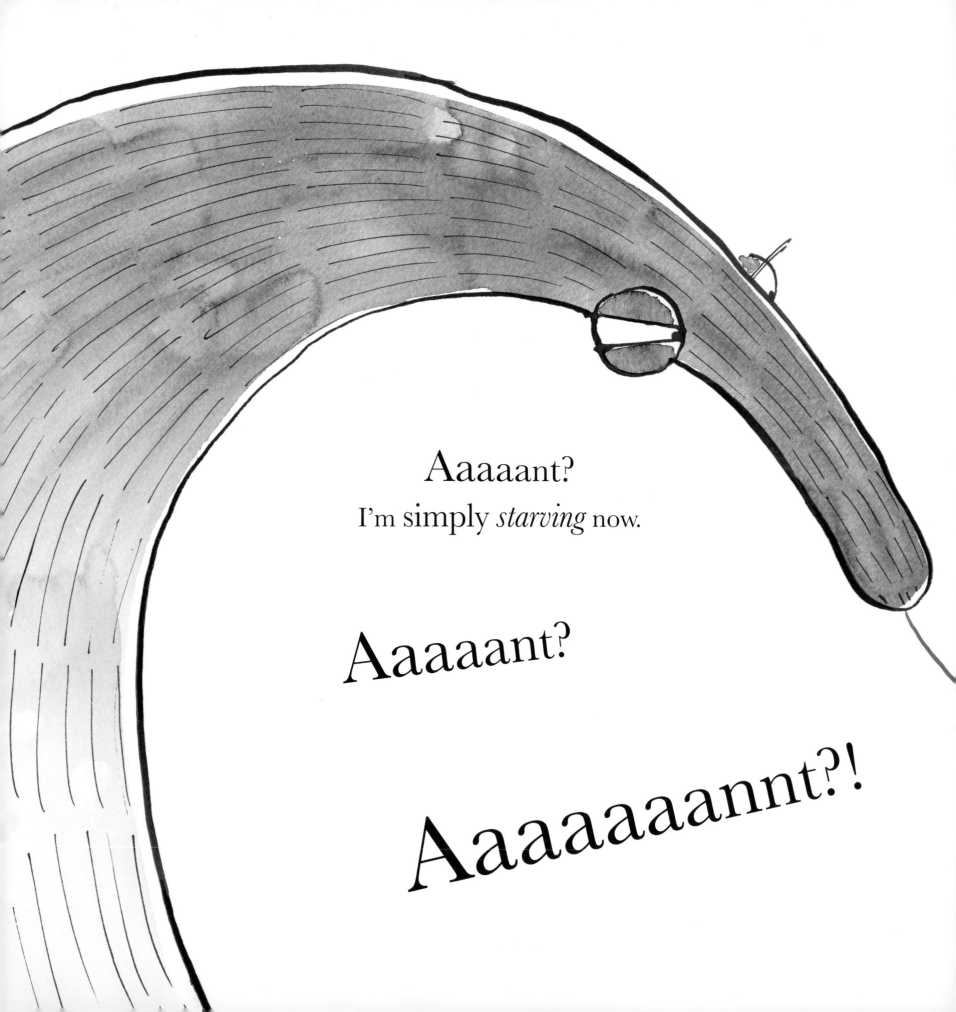

A-ha!
There
you . . .

. . . aaaaaaaarrgghl

"I'm *theriouthly* conthidering
thomething *elth* for thupper!"